THE

HARDY BOYS

Undercover Brothers®

PAPERCUTZ™

THE HARDY BOYS

Undercover Brothers®

#20 *Deadly Strategy*

SCOTT LOBDELL • Writer

PAULO HENRIQUE MARCONDES • Artist

Based on the series by
FRANKLIN W. DIXON

New York

Deadly Strategy
SCOTT LOBDELL — Writer
PAULO HENRIQUE MARCONDES — Artist
LAURIE E. SMITH — Colorist
MARK LERER — Letterer
CHRIS NELSON & CAITLIN HINRICHS — Production
MICHAEL PETRANEK — Editorial Assistant
JIM SALICRUP
Editor-in-Chief

ISBN: 978-1-59707-182-6 paperback edition
ISBN: 978-1-59707-183-3 hardcover edition

Printed in Korea
May 2010 by Tara TPS
192-1 Sangjisuk-ri, Kyoha-eub,
Paju-Si, Kyunggi-do 413-836

Distributed by Macmillan.

10   9   8   7   6   5   4   3   2   1

*A.T.A.C.: *AMERICAN TEENS AGAINST CRIME.*

CHAPTER TWO: "SMASH AND GRAB!"

THE OCEAN OF OSYRIA.

ONE OF THE MIDDLE EAST'S MOST VENERABLE AND VALUABLE JEWELS...

IT IS CURRENTLY ON LOAN TO THE BAYPORT MUSEUM OF INTERNATIONAL ARTS.

WHICH IS ALSO WHERE A REUNION OF SORTS IS TAKING PLACE. FOR IT WAS JOE AND FRANK HARDY WITH HELP FROM FRIENDS CHET MORTON, IOLA MORTON, AND CALLIE SHAW, WHO RECOVERED THE PRECIOUS GEMS AFTER CHET WAS FALSELY ACCUSED OF STEALING THEM.

--WE'LL GET TO THE BOTTOM OF THIS BEFORE YOU CAN SAY--

HUURM.

YEAH, "HURRRM."

THERE'S A SMALL PIECE OF FABRIC HERE ON THE SURFACE.

PROBABLY FROM THE PERSON WHO REMOVED THE OCEAN OF OSYRIA FROM--

UMMM.

ULP.

THIS HAS THE POTENTIAL TO BE VERY BAD.

*SEE HARDY BOYS GRAPHIC NOVEL #17 "WORD UP!"

*SEE HARDY BOYS #14 "HALEY DANIELLE'S TOP EIGHT."

*AS SEEN IN HARDY BOYS #8 "BOARD TO DEATH."

WATCH YOUR STEPS.

YOU KNOW, FRANK-- I'VE ALWAYS THOUGHT I WAS A GLASS FULL KIND OF GUY.

AND NOW?

YAP! YAP!

Poli

EVEN IF WE CAN PROVE THAT THE SISTERS NOIR WERE BEHIND THIS--

--IT'S JUST ONE OF THE CRIMES WE'VE BEEN ACCUSED OF TODAY.

WE'LL FIGURE IT OUT.

SLAM!

*FROM HARDY BOYS #11 "ABRACADEATH."

*SEE HARDY BOYS #15 "LIVE FREE, DIE HARDY!"

*SEE HARDY BOYS #14 "HALEY DANIELLE'S TOP EIGHT"

EPILOGUE: "WHAT YOU CAN"

THE END!

Five years and twenty cases!
Thanks a lot, Joe and Frank—
it's been a blast!
                        —Scott Lobdell

WATCH OUT FOR PAPERCUTZ

We've got good news and bad news for fans of our NANCY DREW and HARDY BOYS graphic novel series. The bad news is that NANCY DREW #21 "High School Musical Mystery Part Two: The Lost Verse" and HARDY BOYS #20 "Deadly Strategy" are the final volumes in each series.

The good news is that Papercutz is proud to announce two new graphic novel series: NANCY DREW THE NEW CASE FILES and THE HARDY BOYS THE NEW CASE FILES.

Confused? Don't be. We decided that after five years of bringing you the best teenage sleuths in our traditional pocket-sized graphic novel format, it was time for an upgrade. The new graphic novel series will be bigger and better than ever. First, we'll be super-sizing our format, jumping up from our current 5" x 7 ½" format to the larger 6" x 9" size, popularized by our CLASSICS ILLUSTRATED and GERONIMO STILTON graphic novels. If you've loved the action-packed pages by Paulo Henrique (with colorist Laurie E. Smith) in HARDY BOYS or the delightfully-designed, anime-like art of Sho Murase in NANCY DREW, you'll love 'em even more at the new size. And it goes without saying that there will be less eye-strain for those of you who scrutinize every little detail on every page.

But that's not all! We know that in the recent Recession, many families have had to cut back on spending, and buying graphic novels can be tough to justify no matter how much you enjoy 'em. That's why the new HARDY BOYS and NANCY DREW graphic novels will be bargain-priced at only $6.99 each. (And of course, don't forget that many Papercutz graphic novels are available at your local library. There's a deal that can't be beat!)

One more bit of good news and bad news. The bad news is that after writing each and every one of the twenty HARDY BOYS graphic novels, our good friend Scott Lobdell is calling it quits. He has so many movie, TV, and publishing projects in the works right now, that something had to give, and unfortunately that something turned out to be THE HARDY BOYS. Let me take this opportunity to thank Scott for not only doing such a great job putting Frank and Joe through their paces in such a dynamic style, but to also thank him for being such a great friend. Time after time, Scott has been there for me when I needed him. Our relationship is a lot like Frank and Joe's, brothers through thick and thin (even though I already have a brother, and Scott has three brothers and three sisters!). While I'm sure we'll all miss Scott's scripts on THE HARDY BOYS, know that Scott's already cooking up ideas for future all-new original Papercutz graphic novel series.

As for the good news…? One of greatest comicbook writers of all time has agreed to write the upcoming HARDY BOYS THE NEW CASE FILES. Just as he was able to step in as writer on *The Amazing Spider-Man* after Stan Lee left, and not miss a beat, but also script such classics as "The Night Gwen Stacy Died," and even create the controversial Punisher, he's now ready to reach new heights of greatness with THE HARDY BOYS. Yes, I'm talking about none other than Gerry Conway! Back when I was Marvel's *Spider-Man* editor, Gerry wrote both *Web of Spider-Man* and *Spectacular Spider-Man*, and created the man called Tombstone, a truly terrifying super-villain. After years of writing such top TV series as *Hercules: The Legendary Journeys* and *Law & Order: Criminal Intent*, Gerry has just recently returned to writing comics, starting with *The Last Days of Animal Man* at DC Comics, and we're super-excited to have him writing THE HARDY BOYS!

On the following pages, we're offering advance peeks at the premiere volumes of both THE HARDY BOYS THE NEW CASE FILES #1 "Crawling with Zombies" and NANCY DREW THE NEW CASE FILES #1 "Vampire Slayer." Now some of you may be shocked to see such super-natural creatures as zombies and vampires entering the relatively realistic world of The Hardy Boys and Nancy Drew. Well, not everything is what it appears to be at first—or is it? Can you determine from the few preview pages provided whether these creatures are real or not? The answers will be revealed in September and October when these two new series debut at your favorite booksellers! So until then, happy sleuthing!

Thanks,

AS A DARK FIGURE LEAPT OVER THE GRAVESTONE I WAS THINKING THIS PROBABLY WOULD HAVE BEEN *MUCH* MORE FRIGHTENING IF I ACTUALLY BELIEVED IN VAMPIRES.

THEN I REALIZED, IT WAS PRETTY MUCH AS FRIGHTENING AS IT COULD GET NO MATTER *WHAT* I BELIEVED.

NANCY DREW
VAMPIRE SLAYER PART ONE

NANCY!

WHAT'S THE PLAN?

RUN!

IT WASN'T ALWAYS MY BEST *PLAN*, BUT IT DID WORK SOMETIMES.

UNLESS WHOEVER WAS CHASING YOU TURNS OUT TO BE MUCH *FASTER*.

I'M GENERALLY *NOT* THE VIOLENT TYPE, BUT IT DIDN'T FEEL LIKE I HAD MUCH CHOICE HERE.

OF COURSE THE CROSSBOW WAS *FAKE*, PART OF MY SLAYER COSTUME.

BUT TALL, DARK, AND *FANGY* HERE DIDN'T KNOW THAT.

MEET BIONICLE ® GRAPHIC NOVELS WRITER
GREG FARSHTEY!

—— A **PAPERCUTZ** Profile ——

We emailed a bunch of questions to the brilliant brain behind the BIONICLE graphic novels, to better get to know this talented writer. Here are the fun-filled, insightful results...

PAPERCUTZ:
When and where were you born?

GREG FARSHTEY: I was born in 1965 in Mount Kisco, NY.

P: What were your favorite toys?

GREG: Mego action figures, and when I was older, LEGO bricks (LEGO bricks didn't come to the US until I was 9). I had a ton of action figures and used to make up stories with them that lasted for months

P: At what age did you start to read?

GREG: I was reading pretty young. I was reading

Shakespeare for fun when I was in first grade, I remember. Plus I learned a lot of vocabulary from comicbooks.

P: What did you read when you were a young boy?

GREG: Comics, especially Batman, Encyclopedia Brown books. The Great Brain books, Sherlock Holmes, and history books.

P: When did you start to write?

GREG: I think the first writing I did was in fourth grade, but I didn't really get serious about it until high school.

P: Who were your favorite writers and artists?

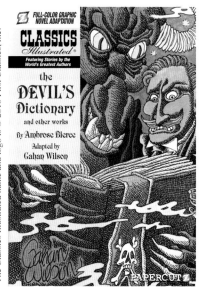

GREG: My favorite writers are Ambrose Bierce, Jeffery Deaver, Raymond Chandler, and most recently, Christopher Fowler. I don't really have favorite artists, though I loved Gene Colan's comicbook work.

P: Did you take any special courses in school to become a writer?

GREG: No. I don't really believe you can teach someone to write. I think you can teach them to read, and to read things that will, in the long run, improve their writing. But I think a lot of writing is instinctive, you can do it or you can't.

P: What was your first published writing?

GREG: I self-published an underground paper in high school, and in college I had a short story published in a literary magazine. The first creative writing I was paid for was a humor column called Town Crier in the first paper I worked at.

P: How did you wind up working on BIONICLE?

GREG: I was hired at the LEGO Company in 2000 as the Club writer, to work on the LEGO Magazine. They were just getting ready to launch BIONICLE then. I knew they were going to do a comic, but figured I was too new to get to do it. I wrote a couple pages just for fun and showed them to my boss. Turned out they needed the first script right away, so I got the chance to do it.

P: Why was the BIONICLE concept ever called "The Bone-Heads of Voodoo Island"?

GREG: Well, I wasn't working on the BIONICLE line at that time, but I suspect that was a combination of placeholder name and code name. Toy and game companies often use code names for projects, just in case the competition gets wind of what you're doing before you release. I once worked on a very, very serious science fiction game whose code name was "Dogs in Space."

P: Did you know when you started writing the BIONICLE stories how sprawling an epic it would become?

GREG: Not really. When I first started working on BIONICLE, the story was largely being dictated to me and I was just adapting it to comics. It really wasn't until the novels started that the universe started to expand.

P: How do you write a BIONICLE story-- what are your working methods?

GREG: Basically, I write it like I do any other fiction -- I let the characters do the heavy lifting. If you create a character the right way, he/she/it becomes like a real person in some ways -- you know what they do and don't like, what they would and wouldn't do, the same way you know that about a friend. Then it becomes easy to know how they would react in a given situation, how they would get along with others or not get along, what would anger them or frighten them. The trick is to not force your character to do something he wouldn't normally do, because at that moment, it becomes impossible to predict his actions and your story grinds to a halt.

P: Which story, in any of the books, comics, or DVDs is your favorite?

GREG: BIONICLE Adventures 10: Time Trap. It's the "smallest" story I have written, in that it really only focuses on two characters, Makuta and

Vakama. It was also the story in which I rebooted Makuta and turned him from a super-villain who always lost to a really complex character who sometimes ALLOWED himself to lose to throw off his opponents.

P: Do you have a favorite BIONICLE character?

GREG: Makuta Teridax and Kopaka. I also like a Dark Hunter named Lariska a lot and the Glatorian named Kiina.

P: Which is your favorite BIONICLE toy? And why?

GREG: I'm not sure I have a favorite set. I tend to like the bigger, more elaborate ones, like the Skopio, because I like longer builds.

P: Do you have a favorite experience meeting BIONICLE fans?

GREG: Yes. I met a young boy named Evan back in 2003, who was a huge BIONICLE fan and had Asperger syndrome. I became close friends with him and his family and we exchanged birthday gifts for years. I am still friends with his Mom and have gotten to see him grow up in photos.

P: What's the best way for BIONICLE fans to contact you?

GREG: Most BIONICLE fans send me questions through a website called BZPower.com, where I am on under the screen name GregF. So that is probably the easiest way to get in touch.

P: Thanks so much, Greg! And keep up the great work!

Don't Miss THE HARDY BOYS THE NEW CASE FILES #1 - "Crawling with Zombies"!